Pete the Popcorn
Plat, Eat, Think, Encourage

Sarviol Publishing
Copyright © Nick Rokicki and Joseph Kelley, 2014

ISBN: 978-1500792688

Special wholesale and re-sale rates are available. For more information,
please contact Deb Harvest at petethepopcorn@gmail.com

When purchasing this book, please consider purchasing
an additional copy to donate to your local library.

THE Pete Popcorn

Play, Eat, Think, Encourage

Written by Nick Rokicki & Joseph Kelley
Illustrated by Ronaldo Florendo

A Note for Parents and Teachers
from co-author Nick Rokicki

In 2012, at a school visit in Michigan, co-author Joe Kelley and I were approached by a student's mother, tears in her eyes. Her son, Tyler, was being bullied because he was overweight. For me, this struck a personal heartstring. Through elementary and high school, I struggled with being the "fat kid" at school. It wasn't easy. In fact, every single day was a struggle. I was called names, I didn't have friends, I had a genuine fear of gym class because I knew I'd be picked last. I knew what Tyler was going through. And I knew we had to do something about it. But it would take time.

I genuinely felt like I couldn't go out and talk to children and families about bullying because of weight, and healthy living, until I made some changes of my own. So, in 2014, I started my journey. Through diet and exercise, I've lost 70 pounds. And now it's time to encourage others to join me--- starting with our child readers.

This book contains some insulting terms, hurled at a character just because she's a little bigger than the other popcorns. These words may come as a shock to some. But I heard them when I was growing up. And I bet Tyler heard them, too. So, after consulting several experts on children's literature, we opted to keep these terms in this story. We did this because this book is meant for two audiences.

The first audience is made up of children and families that are looking for a way to start living healthier lives. While it's not too heavy on specifics, I'm hoping this book might jumpstart or inspire you and the children in your life to practice health.

The second audience are the childhood bullies... the ones that brought tears to the eyes of Tyler's mom. This is where you come in, parents and teachers. When you read this book with the children in your life, please tell them that insulting language towards those of us that may be a little bigger--- is not acceptable. It's hurtful and damaging. If they don't like it that someone might be "fat," instead of hurling names, teach them to become encouragers. Encouragement is the answer.

I'd like to continue this discussion with you, at school visits and speaking engagements nationwide. Please visit us online at www.PeteThePopcorn.com or through www.Facebook.com/PeteThePopcorn. There, you can tell me your story and together we can change this world for the better.

Finally, thank you to Tyler, for inspiring me to be the person I've become.

-Nick Rokicki

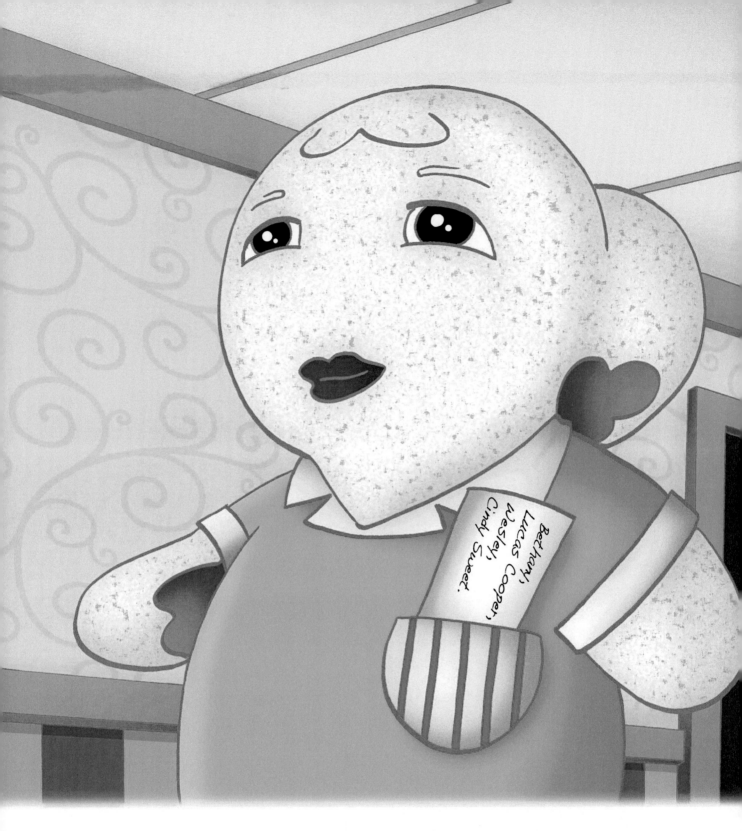

Principal Priscilla Popcorn paced the pathway near the front porch steps of Popcorn Prep. The paperwork for the new student was all prepared, popping out of her polyester pinstripe pocket. Pecky Popcorn had recently moved to Popcorn City from Popcorn Village, where the population was particularly petite.

Soon, a pink Pontiac pulled along Plymouth Parkway. From the passenger side, out stepped a young popcorn, dressed head-to-toe in peach. This must be Pecky Popcorn, thought the principal.

"Welcome to Popcorn Prep," piped Principal Popcorn.

"Hello, my name is Pecky. It is a pleasure to meet you,"
spoke the peaceful popcorn plucking up the path.

"Pecky, that was such a polite introduction. I am pleased to
meet you as well. You'll be so proud to call Popcorn Prep
your new school," praised Principal Popcorn. "Wait here by
the office and I'll be right back to take you to your class."

Just as Principal Popcorn was out of view, Piper Popcorn pushed on around the corner. Piper, wearing a purple polka dotted and padded headband, was one of Popcorn Prep's most popular and pesky popcorns.

"Well, this must be the new pop-girl in town," pouted Piper, with a plotting look on her face. "I didn't think you'd be such a puffy and downright porky popcorn. I better get to lunch promptly— before YOU partake and pig out!"

Principal Popcorn passed the office just as Piper was pouncing away. She saw the panicked look on Pecky's face and promised, "Perk up, princess! Everything will be ok. I know new schools can be a pain, but all of the popcorns here at Popcorn Prep are in pursuit of being painstakingly proper."

Pecky Popcorn fought back tears. She didn't want to be a tattle-tale on her first day at Popcorn Prep. The plucky popcorn took a deep breath and proceeded with Principal Popcorn down the passage, plastered with projects that other popcorns had perfected.

Promptly, they arrived at a door, which Principal Popcorn pulled open. "Professor Popcorn? Pupils? May I have your attention? This is your new classmate, Pecky Popcorn," pronounced the principal. "Please treat her with respect and dignity as you welcome her into Popcorn Prep!"

"Welcome, welcome!" exclaimed Professor Popcorn. "Go ahead and have a seat in the middle there. Right at that empty desk."

As Pecky made her way to the seat, she felt relief as she peered at the popcorns in front of her. A pop-boy and a pop-girl, they were both smiling profoundly.

"Hi! My name is Patty," explained the girl.

"And my name is Pete," bellowed the boy.

Pecky enjoyed the rest of the morning, as Pete and Patty introduced her to the popcorns in her class, showed her around Popcorn Prep and answered every question she had. Pecky couldn't wait for recess... swinging on the swings was her favorite activity!

Pete, Patty and Pecky were pounding the pavement, making their way towards the swings. Suddenly, three popcorns paraded in front of them, not permitting them to the playground. In the middle position stood Piper Popcorn.

"Those swings might have a problem holding you, pudgy. I presume there is a poundage limit for potbelly piglets like you," pointed out Piper. Pecky immediately turned, running back towards the school building. Patty chased after her.

"Piper Popcorn! You positively know better than to speak like that! Words hurt more than you can imagine! Percy, you and Polly need to talk to your friend," insisted Pete, addressing the three popcorns in front of him. "If you don't stop, I am parading down and speaking with Principal Popcorn."

At lunch, Pete and Patty sat down with Pecky. "I don't know why she's being so mean— I can't help it that I'm bigger than all the other popcorns! It's just who I am!" confessed Pecky.

"You shouldn't pay any attention to what Piper Popcorn has to say! All you can do is be the healthiest popcorn YOU can be!" pronounced Patty.

"But I don't know how, Patty. I eat the things I like to eat," complained Pecky.

"Being healthy isn't just about eating, Pecky. Eating food is something we all do to live every day," added Pete. "But you can learn to like new foods— and eat other foods just sometimes. It's really easy if you think about it!"

"Pete is right— just look at his name! We can turn it into an acronym! P.E.T.E. Play, Eat, Think, Encourage!" proclaimed Patty. Through the next few weeks, Patty demonstrated to Pecky exactly what she meant...

"When you really think about it, exercise is just playing! Take this pogo stick— you can jump on it for just 20 minutes and get plenty of good exercise, while you have some fun," offered Patty.

"Or even riding your bike!" boasted Pete. "We could ride our bikes to and from school every day, instead of taking the bus. Not only would it be a plethora of fun, we could all talk about our school day and we'd be playing— I mean, exercising!"

"Well, then what about eating?" asked Pecky.

"I'll tell you what, Pecky... why don't I have Poppa
pack your lunch tomorrow, too? He always makes mine
really healthy— and delicious!" mentioned Patty.

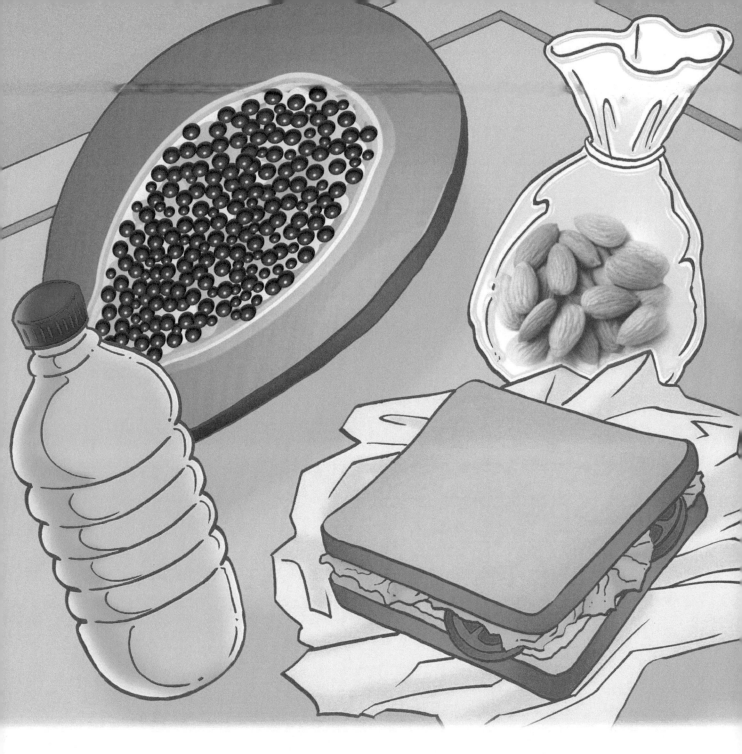

The next day, Patty pranced up to the picnic table at Popcorn Prep with two parcels of food. Opening the package for Pecky, she produced a papaya, a small bag of almonds, a bottle of water, and even a sandwich— made with lettuce!

Pecky protested, "Oh, Patty... I don't like lettuce!"

"You've got to try new things, Pecky! There's some more surprises on there," remarked Patty.

Pecky focused at Patty and Pete, closed her eyes, and took a bite. The crunch of the lettuce was matched with the crunch of something else! What was that? Carrots! Carrots on the sandwich added some sweetness!

"This is so good, Patty! I never knew I liked vegetables! But Momma Popcorn says fresh fruit and vegetables are too expensive. I don't know if I can eat like this every day," said Pecky.

"Poppa makes plans to go to plenty of farmer's markets practically every single week! It's where farmers bring their homegrown produce and sell it to all of us popcorns, right from the farm!" said Patty. "Not only do you get a great deal, but you know you're eating fresh food that came from just miles away!"

"This all seems so easy, Patty. What did the 'T' stand for in your P.E.T.E. acronym?" quizzed Pecky.

"Actually," interjected Pete, "that's the easiest one of all. It just means that you should think every single day about your goals and your health. Think about how much playing you've done that day. Think about what you've eaten. Think about what you're going to do tomorrow!"

"And the 'E' is what Pete and I are doing right now!" hinted Patty. "We are encouraging others to live like we do! The easiest way to spread the word about how easy you can become healthy, is for you to help others learn how and encourage them to stay on track. Some popcorns, like Piper, don't understand that encouragement is the key for us all to become better popcorns!"

Months passed by and Pecky adored her new school, new friends and new healthy life! One day, she peeked around herself at the picnic table. Of course, she saw Pete and Patty. But now Percy and Polly were sitting with them, too. Pecky looked past the play area and saw Piper, perched on the ground underneath the Pear tree, picking petunias.

"Piper always called me the bigger popcorn... perhaps now is the time to prove her right," declared Pecky. She walked across the courtyard, approaching Piper. "I know we've never gotten along. Or even talked at all. But I wanted to see if you'd like to come sit at our table. It can't be too comfortable on the ground."

Principal Priscilla Popcorn and Professor Popcorn watched from afar as the popcorns had a pep in their step and pranced together towards the picnic table. "Sometimes, these little popcorns can solve their own problems," panted Professor Popcorn.

Principal Popcorn proposed, "Perhaps all it takes is a pint-sized bit of encouragement."

DID YOU KNOW???

Every book by Joe Kelley and Nick Rokicki contains "secrets" hidden in the illustrations! We enjoy meeting our kid fans at school readings and events nationwide, where we share these. These secrets are always a nod to future books--- or some of our past books.

Although there are LOTS of secrets in this book, we'd like to share ONE:

**LOOK CLOSE!
SEE THOSE PUMPKINS?**

These are included at the fruit and vegetable market because our next book in the Pete the Popcorn series is Pete the Popcorn: Popcorns, Pumpkins and Purpose! Look for it starting in Fall of 2015.

THINK YOU KNOW A SECRET?
ASK US ON FACEBOOK!

facebook

WWW.FACEBOOK.COM/PETETHEPOPCORN

OUR OTHER BOOKS!

PETE THE POPCORN IS AN AMAZON BESTSELLER! TEACHES CHILDREN TO ENCOURAGE EACH OTHER EVERY SINGLE DAY!

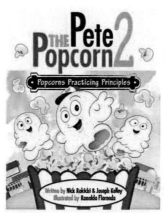

PETE THE POPCORN: POPCORNS PRACTICING PRINCIPLES IS ALL ABOUT HONESTY! FIND OUT WHAT HAPPENS WHEN PETE FINDS A POCKETBOOK

CASEY AND CALLIE CUPCAKE IS A FROSTED FABLE ABOUT BEING FANTASTIC JUST THE WAY YOU ARE!

CRUSTY CUPCAKE'S HAPPY BIRTHDAY: FRIENDSHIPS LAST FOREVER IS ABOUT A CUPCAKE BIRTHDAY PARTY THAT GOES WRONG!

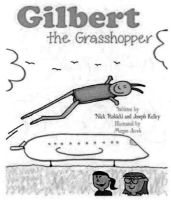

GILBERT THE GRASSHOPPER IS A CROSSOVER BOOK FOR CHILDREN TO GAIN CONFIDENCE TO BEGIN READING CHAPTER BOOKS!

FIRST PHOTO OF THE ROYAL BABY TEACHES KIDS THAT A SIMPLE SMILE CROSSES ALL LANGUAGES!

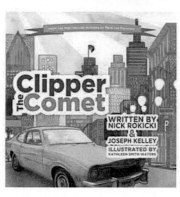

CLIPPER THE COMET, SET IN A SMALL MICHIGAN TOWN, GIVES CREDIT TO FAMILIES THAT MADE THE MOTOR CITY OF DETROIT. LESSONS IN HARD WORK AND FAMILY ABOUND.

Made in the USA
Middletown, DE
01 April 2016